EXTREME
SPORTS
An Imagination Library Series

ROCK CLIMBING

by John E. Schindler

GARETH**STEVENS**
GS
PUBLISHING
A WRC Media Company

Please visit our web site at: www.garethstevens.com
For a free color catalog describing Gareth Stevens Publishing's
list of high-quality books and multimedia programs,
call 1-800-542-2595 (USA) or 1-800-387-3178 (Canada).
Gareth Stevens Publishing's fax: (414) 332-3567.

Library of Congress Cataloging-in-Publication Data

Schindler, John E.
   Rock climbing / by John E. Schindler.
      p. cm. — (Extreme sports: an imagination library series)
   Includes bibliographical references and index.
   ISBN 0-8368-4541-2 (lib. bdg.)
   ISBN 0-8368-4548-X (softcover)
   1. Rock climbing—Juvenile literature. I. Title. II. Extreme sports (Milwaukee, Wis.)
GV200.2.S35   2005
796.522'3—dc22   2004062579

First published in 2005 by
Gareth Stevens Publishing
A WRC Media Company
330 West Olive Street, Suite 100
Milwaukee, WI 53212 USA

Text: John E. Schindler
Cover design and page layout: Tammy West
Series editor: Carol Ryback
Photo research: Diane Laska-Swanke

Photo credits: Cover, pp. 5, 11 © Christian Perret/Jump; pp. 7, 21 © www.guntermarx-stockphotos.com;
pp. 9, 17, 19 © Howie Garber/Wanderlust Images; pp. 13, 15 © Jeremiah Watt

Printed in the United States of America

1 2 3 4 5 6 7 8 9 09 08 07 06 05

Cover: A rock climber high on a lake bluff looks for a toe hold. The rope hooked to her rock climbing gear helps keep her safe.

TABLE OF CONTENTS

Words that appear in the glossary are printed in **boldface** type the first time they occur in the text.

ROCK CLIMBING

Rock climbing is not just a grown-up sport anymore. Kids like you often join in the fun. Climbing rocks makes your muscles stronger. You can become more **flexible**.

Pretend you are hanging off of a rock wall. The view up there is great. You might see over the treetops. You might see a train far away. You might look down and see the tops of your friends' heads!

How can you learn to rock climb? Where can you try it? What kind of gear will you need? Keep turning these pages for the answers.

An instructor looks down at his group of rock climbing students. They are learning how to follow each other up a rock wall.

WALLS THAT ROCK

You can rock climb almost anywhere!

An indoor climbing gym is a great place to start. Climbing gyms have walls that look like rock. They can be easy or hard to climb.

Most climbing gyms offer rock climbing lessons. Your rock climbing teacher will show you how to build up your strength. You will learn all about climbing safety.

Someday you might climb an inside rock wall. Do not bang your head on the ceiling!

Some rock climbing schools bring the rock walls to you! One young girl listens to instructions while another climbs up a movable wall.

WHAT HOLDS YOUR TOES?

Do you need special clothes to climb rocks? No! Just wear clothes that let you move easily.

Rock climbing shoes are a different story. Climbers must think about what they put their feet on. They must also think about what they put on their feet. Rock climbers match their shoes to the type of rock they will climb.

Climbing shoes are made to grip rock. Indoor rock climbing shoes do not work as well on outdoor rocks. Shoes for outdoor rocks are tougher.

You must wear a helmet when you rock climb. A helmet protects your head from falling rocks. The helmet also makes you look cool!

8

These climbers wear climbing shoes but regular clothes. What safety gear are they missing? If you said helmets, you are right!

GEARING UP

Rock climbing ropes are strong but stretchy. They help stop you from falling all the way down. Ropes let you keep climbing even if you slip.

You must learn to tie many kinds of knots for rock climbing. One of the knots is called a figure eight knot. It makes the rope look like the number eight.

You attach a rope to your safety **harness**. The safety harness goes around your waist. A special metal clip called a **carabiner** attaches the harness to your safety rope. Carabiners come in many shapes and sizes.

Rock climbers check each other's knots before a climb.

UP YOU GO!

Free-climbing is the general name for a few different ways to climb rocks. In free-climbing, the rope does not pull you up. It is only hooked to your harness to keep you from falling all the way down.

Top roping is a very safe kind of free-climbing. An **anchor** at the very top of the climb holds the rope tightly. A safety person at the bottom of the climb holds the lower end of the rope.

The safety person watches you climb. He or she is called a **belayer**. If you slip, the belayer can pull on the rope and stop your fall.

The girl at the bottom holds the top rope for the climber up above. She is the belayer. She will help keep her climbing partner from falling far.

TAKING THE LEAD

Experienced rock climbers can climb mountains or very high cliffs. These climbers cannot use a top rope to help them. Instead, they carry the rope up the rock wall. Taking the rope up a rock wall is called **lead climbing**.

The lead climber carries more than his rope. He also carries **bolts**. He puts the bolts into the **rock face** as he climbs. The rope goes through the holes of the bolts.

Other climbers use special equipment to help them climb. They are called **technical** climbers.

Rock climbers can climb the highest mountains in the world using lead and technical climbing.

A lead climber reaches toward a hook with his rope. The hook was left by an earlier climber.

GOING SOLO

Climbing without a rope is called **free soloing**. Only the very best climbers can free solo.

A free solo climber uses only her hands and feet to climb a rock wall. She carries a bag full of chalk dust on her belt. She puts chalk dust on her hands to keep them from slipping when she grabs the rock.

Solo climbers often climb up narrow rock openings called **chimneys**. To climb a chimney, the solo climber pushes against both sides of the chimney. He uses his back, legs, and arms to climb a chimney.

Free soloing is the most dangerous type of rock climbing. Free solo climbers are amazing **athletes**.

Free solo rock climbing is often very dangerous. A solo climber must know exactly how to climb without help or ropes.

LOOK OUT BELOW!

What goes up must come down — even if it is you! Climbing down can be harder than climbing up. Sometimes, climbers find a way to walk down to where they began. Other times, climbers slowly and carefully climb down the rock wall.

Can you think of a way to get down faster?

Climbers know how to drop down very fast. They slide down their top ropes! Dropping down the rope is called **rappelling**. It is fast and fun. Some people think rappelling is the best part of rock climbing!

A climber gets ready to rappel down a cliff that is next to a waterfall.

YOU DID IT!

One of the biggest thrills of rock climbing is getting to the top. It is fun to be high above everything. The hard work of climbing up is well worth the effort!

Some people climb for the view. Some people climb for the exercise. Some people climb because it makes them feel good to get to the top. Everyone has a different reason.

What will your reason be? You'll have to learn to rock climb to find out!

What a view! A climber enjoys what she sees after reaching the top of a rock wall.

MORE TO READ AND VIEW

Books (Nonfiction) *Rock Climbing. Kids' Guides to the Outdoors* (series). Tim Seeberg. (Child's World)

Rock Climbing. Cover-To-Cover Informational Books (series). Mike Graf. (Perfect Learning)

Sport Climbing. Extreme Sports (series). Edward Voeller. (Capstone)

Extreme Climbing. Extreme Sports No Limits! (series). John Crossingham. (Crabtree)

Rock Climbing. Radical Sports (series). Neil Champion. (Heinemann)

Extreme Rock Climbing Moves. Behind the Moves (series). Kathleen W. Deady. (Capstone)

Books (Fiction) *Rock On. The Extreme Team #5* (series). Matt Christopher. (Little, Brown)

DVDs and Videos *Beyond Gravity.* (Black and White Productions)

Inertia 1 & 2 Rock Climbing. (Integrity 7 Productions)

22

WEB SITES

Web sites change frequently, but the following web sites should last awhile. You can also search Google (*www.google.com*) or Yahooligans! (*www.yahooligans.com*) for more information about rock climbing. Some keywords to help your search include: *abseiling, bouldering, climbing calls, climbing moves, rappelling, rock climbing grades and class, rock climbing knots.*

alumnus.caltech.edu/~sedwards/ climbing/techniques.html
See diagrams of the various types of climbing techniques. Follow links to other information on rock climbing.

online.sector.sk/hra.aspx?game =786
Try your luck with an online rock climbing game. Use your mouse to move the climber's hands and feet. Help the climber get to the top without falling.

www.adventuregallery.net/Kennan _Harvey/frames/rock_climbing_ pictures.php?contentPage=page005 &navID=K-005
View some really cool rock climbing pictures online.

www.ehow.com/how_11864_ buy-helmet-rock.html
Learn how to choose the right climbing helmet to stay safe. Explore links to other information on rock climbing.

GLOSSARY

You can find these words on the pages listed. Reading a word in a sentence helps you understand it even better.

anchor — a strong support. 12

athletes — people who like to do sports. 16

belayer — a safety person at the bottom of a rock wall who can pull on the climbing rope to stop a climber from falling. 12

bolts — metal pegs with a loop at one end. 14

carabiner (care-a-BEE-ner) — a metal clip used to hook rock climbing ropes together. 10

chimneys — narrow openings between two rock walls. 16

flexible — able to bend easily. 4

free-climbing — climbing while using only a rope for safety. 12, 16

free soloing — climbing without a rope. 16

harness — a set of straps used for support. 10, 12

lead climbing — carrying a rope and placing anchors while climbing up a rock wall. 14

rappelling — coming down off a rock face by sliding down a rope. 18

rock face — the wall of rock facing you. 14

technical — very difficult rock climbing. 14

top roping — climbing with an anchored rope. 12, 18

INDEX